FIRE! FIRE!

CONTENTS

FIRE! FIRE!

Fire is frightening.
It can burn huge forests.
It can burn homes and buildings.
Fire can spread quickly
if it is not stopped.

3

FIGHTING FIRE

Firefighters are trained
to put out fires.
They are trained to handle
all sorts of emergencies.
They may be called to huge
forest fires or car crashes.

Firefighters have fire engines and special gear to help them deal with fires in all sorts of places. They learn how to use this gear. They practise putting out fires.

Firefighters have to be ready
to fight fires at any time.
The fire engines are ready to go
as soon as the alarm sounds.
The firefighters arrange their gear
so they can get into it quickly.

In some countries, fire engines
are now yellow, white, or green.
These colours are easier to see
at night than red.

THE PUMP APPLIANCE

The pump appliance is the most important part of a fire engine. It lets the firefighters pump water from the fire hydrants. The rush of water is so strong that it takes at least two or three firefighters to hold the fire hose.

11

THE HOOK AND LADDER

A hook-and-ladder engine is very long. In some countries, it is so long there is a driver for the front and a driver for the back. The ladders are folded up and can be extended to help fight fires in tall buildings.

FIRE BOATS AND HELICOPTERS

Sometimes firefighters fight fires from fire boats. Fire boats pump the water from a river or the ocean onto the fires.

Helicopters are also used to fight fires. They dump huge buckets of water onto a fire.

15

FIGHTING FIRES WITHOUT WATER

Gas and oil fires cannot be put out with water. These fires are put out with foam or dry chemicals that are sprayed onto the fire with a fire extinguisher. The foam smothers the fire and puts it out.

FIGHTING FIRES LONG AGO

Long ago, people did not have fire hydrants to help them fight fires. People would form a "bucket brigade" to bring water to the fire.

The first fire engines were pulled by horses. The first motorized fire engines had bells to warn people to get out of the way.

FIRE AT HOME

All homes should have smoke detectors to warn people of fire. You should always have a plan for getting out of your house.

If you are caught in a fire:
- try not to panic
- never try to hide
- get outside quickly.

If your clothes ever catch on fire, remember: **stop**, **drop**, **roll**.

Fire needs air to stay alight. You can smother a small fire with a mat or a rug, or put it out with a fire extinguisher.

21

ACCIDENTS HAPPEN EASILY

Remember:

- Never play with matches or lighters.
- Never play with toasters, stoves, or ovens.
- Always have an adult present when you are around a fire.
- Always make sure that campfires and candles are put out before you leave or go to bed.
- Always wear sensible clothing and shoes when you are around a fire.

INDEX